Trail of the Hunter

Jack Gannon

Cyndi Williams-Barnier

For Permission requests, write to:

YBR Publishing, LLC
PO Box 4904
Beaufort SC 29903-4904
contact@ybrpub.com
843-900-0859

ISBN-13: 979-8-9852082-3-8

YBR PUBLISHING, LLC

Jack Gannon – Co-Owner, Production Manager
Cyndi Williams-Barnier - Co-Owner, Marketing Manager
Bill Barnier – Co-Owner, Senior Editor
Loreen Ridge-Husum – Art Director

REVIEWS

4-STAR AWARD

Reviewed By Rolanda Lyles for Readers' Favorite, LLC

Harold, a scientist on the hunt for Bigfoot, has gone missing in the forests of northwest Washington State. Task Force Agent Hunter, accompanied by Cat Whisker Margaux Martell, has been dispatched to find him, not realizing the dangers awaiting them on their search. While Hunter has a history with Harold, she is skeptical about the belief in Bigfoot. She just wants to find her old friend. Hunter has keen tracking and hunting abilities to find anybody and Whisker Margaux, well, her abilities are a bit supernatural, but an asset to their unlikely team. Their boss thought the pair would make a great team, and they will soon discover why. While searching for Harold, they realize that they are being followed, but who is their elusive stalker and what does he want with them?

Jack Gannon and Cyndi Williams-Barnier's "Trail of the Hunter"…is a fast-paced story full of action and suspense. While brief, the authors quickly jump into the plot of the story with the agents getting acquainted and heading out undercover to find the missing scientist. Gannon and Williams-Barnier also took great care to give some history and backstory on the main characters so that readers could connect to both the characters and the plot. It is a story full of fantastic characters, twists, turns, and an unsuspected ending. Jack Gannon and Cyndi Williams-Barnier's "Trail of the Hunter" is sure to knock your socks off and is a must-read for all those who enjoy action and adventure tales.

AUTHORS' NOTE

The flashback scene on pages 26-27 is from "2s And 3s", also by the authors.

CHAPTER 1

"HELLO AND GOODBYE"

Mae-Lei Komala, the Task Force Division agent code-named "Hunter", strode purposefully down the hallway, the heels of her brown leather boots thumped on the tiled floor as she walked. She approached her office within the Task Force Division's headquarters just outside of Washington, D.C., stopped and waited for the optical reader and fingerprint scanner at her office door to accept her identity. The stainless-steel door clicked, unlocked and silently slid open, disappearing into the wall. Once inside, she activated the door keypad panel, pushing a button that ordered the door to stay open.

The native-Hawaiian agent pulled two large travel bags from her equipment closet, her jet-black waist length hair falling forward, getting in the way. She pulled her hair back, knotting it into a ponytail without the need of a hair clip. She set the bags on a table near her desk, then stepped over to her weapons wall to peruse the collection, trying to decide which ones to take on her mission. The weapons display was massive; from floor to ceiling, it contained usable weapons of all shapes, sizes, and varieties collected from her global travels. Other walls contained weapons and similar paraphernalia as well, but their purpose was merely for display. Some she'd dug up at archeology finds, dating back thousands of years, others were ancient or outdated, mostly gifts from friends. First walking into her office, it smelled musky, old and dirt-like, yet one also felt as if they'd stepped into a museum showcasing ancient relics.

Her arms were crossed and her back to the door as she pondered when a knock on the wall by her open door ended her concentration. "Mae?" fellow agent Harri "Proteus" Lewis asked.

Mae-Lei replied politely, "Hey, Harri."

The petite blond agent stepped into the office, eyeing the open bags on the table. "So, you taking a trip? Got a new mission already?"

"Yep," Mae-Lei replied.

Harri immediately picked up on the bad vibes. "There's a problem…with your mission?"

Mae-Lei turned and stared at the young agent, lids narrowed, and brow furrowed. She cocked her head to the side and said, "You're very perceptive." She moved to her desk, sliding her slim, five-foot seven-inch body up onto the edge. "Not so much a problem as a concern or worry. My mission is to find a missing Smithsonian scientist, who also happens to be on the payroll here from time to time as an extremely valuable consultant, but more important, a very dear friend."

"You're the right agent for the job," Harri said.

"I agree." Both women smiled at the modest humor. "Professor Harold Windimer was my geology, geography, and anthropology professor when I was in college before I enlisted in the Army." Her legs dangled off the desk, and she crossed her ankles. "And, we got to be, well…good friends, for a while, that is."

"Ah," Harri replied knowingly. "You've a bit more personal incentive to succeed."

Mae-Lei nodded. "But Harold was several years before I met Marshall here," Mae-Lei said, referring to her late fiancé and prior Task Force field team leader. "We stayed in touch over the years after we stopped being a couple, as his research took him across the world. Our paths never did seem to cross again, though, except when he was called in to help us on a case." She tinkered with some paper clips on her desktop as she spoke. "So, anyway, he took off on vacation recently and it seems like he suddenly dropped off the face of the planet. He's pretty much irreplaceable, the things he knows, and the detailed work he does for us. He has knowledge of things that no one else in the world knows about—kinda priceless, I guess."

"Where do you start?" Angela asked as she leaned against the wall.

"Seattle." Mae-Lei studied the weapons wall for a few more seconds. She slid back to her feet, walked over and removed two handguns from the wall to put in a bag, instinctively checking to make sure they were unloaded…for the time being. She turned to her left and reached for a sheathed machete. "He apparently went on a, sort of," she said, stretching high on tiptoes, grunting a bit to reach the weapon, "wildlife hunt and disappeared shortly after leaving the city." Mae-Lei walked to her uniform closet and removed a green uniform, in the same style as the standard black field uniform and placed it in a bag. "I'm going off-road, so a safari vehicle is being prepped for me." She stopped and looked at Angela. "Are you familiar with the Cat Whiskers?"

Harri smiled, knowingly. "Of course," she replied. "I've spent a good bit of time over in that department at Mark's company, observing, and learning while in my Deborah O'Bannon guise. That was a research group Mark's grandpa started at Jason Enterprises. He picked out people who claimed to be clairvoyant, sensitive, psychic, that kinda stuff, and tested them for accuracy in their respective claimed abilities. There are actually some really sophisticated training programs that go on over there now."

"Training? Well, for the last few months your dad has formed them into some, what, I don't know, special Task Force operations unit. I've just never been a believer in ESP and all that other crap." Mae-Lei rubbed her temples. "And I can't believe I'm saying this, but they've actually been helpful on occasion with some smaller Task Force assignments, but don't you tell a soul I just admitted that." She took a deep breath. "It's just so hard to believe in their hocus-pocus act."

Harri crossed her arms. "No problem. But don't you believe in your own native deities?"

Mae-Lei looked up at her, a questioning look in her eyes.

"Your own kapu should make you more accepting of others' talents besides your own, even if you don't agree with them." Harri smiled innocently, then added, "I spent some time on Oahu when I was active-duty."

Mae-Lei laughed. "You're right, of course. Okay, my aumakua is now telling me you already have an idea to help me get started a little faster, and it would be in my best interest to listen."

"Come on over to my little hole," Harri invited her. She led Mae-Lei to her office just down the hall. After opening the door, Harri led her inside; the office walls were adorned in various latex face masks used as disguises on missions, padded clothing to change physical appearances, and more. Harri was the team's special effects chief as well as tactical expert.

"Because the professor has Task Force credentials, his cell phone GPS is automatically tagged into a spy satellite network to track his moves, no matter where he went. I don't know if he's aware of that or not, do you?" Harri pressed a few more commands into her keyboard, and the image took over all four screens. She adjusted the resolution until it was obvious that his heat signature was in a forest area. A further adjustment revealed his heat signature as a human and other heat signatures were obvious forest creatures: birds, rodents, wolves, and such.

"Everyone connected with TF is passively monitored by automation where they go, yes."

Harri increased the image speed. Hours' worth of time passed in minutes as the satellite followed his trek through the trees, as he stopped to examine the ground one spot after another.

She suddenly stopped the forward speed and returned it to normal time. The heat-resolution image showed the professor's form alone, with absolutely no wildlife nearby. Without warning, a larger human figure appeared from the foliage and approached the professor. The professor's image began running away with the second image in pursuit, the second quickly caught up to the professor, and for a few moments the two were intertwined before their combined heat image just as quickly winked out. "What the hell?" Mae-Lei gasped. "Can you get any better resolution on that scene; get some kinda detail on who that was? Man, there's so many trees." Harri resumed the rapid time-passage on the screen from all angles, 3-D included, as the satellite remained focused on that section of geography for three days' time.

"That was the best image possible, considering it was shot through a forest from geocentric orbit without real-time human manipulation." Angela pressed another set of commands, and Mae-Lei's cell phone beeped. "I just sent you his last coordinates from his phone; it's still active and connected to GPS. He must've dropped it during those last few seconds, which is why the satellite locator remains fixed on that location. You've at least got a place to start."

"Bonjour," a heavily French-accented voice said from behind them. They turned around to look at a slightly shorter woman than Harri, with short brown hair, large round glasses, and dressed in a midnight-blue version of the Task Force black field uniform. She had a black backpack slung over her shoulders. "Agent Hunter? I am Margaux Martell, Cat Whisker Department, reporting for duty."

Mae-Lei, with an eyebrow raised, looked at the newcomer, then at Harri, and then back at Margaux. She took a deep cleansing breath and asked, "And just what is your talent, Miss Martell?"

"S'il vous plaît, I am classified as a sensitive, mademoiselle," she replied in slow, broken English. "I divine information from my surroundings." She handed Mae-Lei a flash drive. "My file."

Mae-Lei took it and passed it to Harri, who inserted it into the server port. After typing in two security passwords, the file opened on the bottom left screen, and the two Task Force agents read the information that scrolled up. They looked at each other, then back at the Cat Whisker.

"I can't wait to read your report when you get back, Agent Hunter." They both looked back at the confidential file on the screen. "Hol-eee shit," Harri said in a whisper.

"No shit," said Mae-Lei. She stood tall and looked at Margaux. "You better be as good as this report says you are."

"I shall do my best, mademoiselle."

Mae-Lei crossed her arms. "Call me 'Hunter'. I'm not a 'mademoiselle'. Do you have a field name?"

"No, ma'am."

"'Chocolate'," said Harri, jumping to the challenge unbidden. "Her field name needs to be 'Chocolate'." Mae-Lei looked at Angela quizzically. "Don't you get it? Margaux Martell—M and M—like the candy?"

"Oh, sweet," Mae-Lei said sarcastically, rolling her eyes in disbelief at the terrible pun. "Okay, Agent Choc-o-late, we're gonna haul ass to Washington in one hour. And go get a different color uniform for forest infiltration, and the non-scented bug spray, we're gonna be blending into the trees on this mission." Mae-Lei escorted the Whisker out of Angela's office.

"Sweet, indeed," said Harri.

CHAPTER 2

"UP, UP, AND AWAY"

Margaux found Hunter at the Task Force hangar on Andrews Air Force Base. Hunter was dressed in jeans and a University of Hawaii T-shirt and black sneakers, not in the normal field uniform agents wore on a mission, checking the inventory already packed in the safari vehicle before it was loaded in the transport bay. Hunter observed that Margaux was still dressed in her blue uniform. "You know," said Hunter, "you are allowed to wear civilian clothes."

"Yes, ma'am," Margaux replied, "but I didn't know if protocol allowed them en route to a mission. But I do have a change of clothing in my backpack."

"Go ahead and change once we're inside the plane then. Is this your first time in the field on assignment?" Hunter asked.

"Oui."

"Ever ride in an airplane?"

"Oui."

"Ever get airsick?"

"Ah, no, ma'am, never."

"Good. Don't need a Cat Whisker barfing up hairballs the whole trip," Hunter said dryly. "So just how did you get picked for this mission?"

Margaux searched for the correct words in English. "I was told by Ma--Spy that my abilities were a perfect match for you."

"Oh, he did, did he?" Hunter said calmly, leaning against the jeep. "I look forward to testing your 'matched' abilities when we get started."

"As do I, Agent Hunter."

"Just 'Hunter', no need to be that formal. We're going to be together for quite a while." She placed a gentle hand on Margaux's shoulder. "Go on up and get settled in the sleeping compartments and change into something casual. I'll be up as soon as I'm finished here and get this thing loaded into the TF plane."

Margaux nodded and went to the stairs leading to the fuselage.

Once she finished verifying her equipment, Hunter put her weapons bag in the safari, slung her personal bag over her shoulder and gave the ground crew a "thumbs up" signal that they could load the vehicle into the belly of the transport. Following Margaux into the passenger area of the plane, she made a call on her cell phone. "Anna? Mae…yeah, I'm off on another business trip, how'd you know? Right, airplanes in the background here… Thank you, I really appreciate it. Daddy says your bonsai is almost ready to deliver to you…No, honestly, he feels it's his duty to give all my close friends a clipping from his family bonsai, especially the ones who help me…This fall, he promises…Thanks, dear…yes, we'll have wine and talk about my trip when I get back. See you in a few days…Bye."

She hung up with her best girl friend and neighbor, and remembered...

▲

SEVENTEEN YEARS AGO

Kilohani Komala was sitting in his wicker chair on the back porch of their home outside Hilo, Hawaii, nearest the family's antique hand-carved Tiki god. On the patio table beside him was his favorite intricately grown bonsai tree, one of the many he'd cultured for years in the house. Seventeen-year-old Mae-Lei kissed her mother good morning, poured a cup of coffee, and joined him outside in the perfect Hawaiian spring weather. While he wore khaki slacks, a flowered shirt, and sandals, she wore only a long T-shirt. She propped her long, tanned legs up on a chair seat as she sat beside him, her red toenails glistening in the morning sun. "Good morning, Daddy," she said.

"Good morning, Mae," he replied. "Don't you think you should have more on before Lani gets here?"

Mae-Lei laughed. "He has seen me in much less, Daddy."

"Bah, I don't need to hear things like that!" He held up a hand while holding a newspaper in the other.

"My bikini! What, do you think we skinny-dip on a public beach?"

Kilohani grinned. "Would not surprise me if you did."

"Daddy! Really!" Mae-Lei laughed as she took another sip of her coffee.

Kilohani took a deep breath. "So, have you told him yet?"

"No," she said softly. "I haven't worked up the nerve yet."

"Well, if you're going to join the army you'll have to work on that nerve. They'll send you to duty stations across the world, even places where women aren't looked upon as property or worse."

"If you're trying to scare me into not going," she said, "it's not working."

"Mae, no," he replied, "I want you to go! You've always talked about traveling and seeing new places…making a difference somewhere. Who knows, you might even find a husband out there."

"Daddy, c'mon now. What makes you think I'll find someone to replace Lani?"

"Because," he replied, "you don't love Lani." He stared at her over his bifocals. "You just like being with him. But," he added as he leaned toward her, "you don't love him, while he loves you. Now don't deny it, a father can see these things." He pointed at the bonsai beside him. "This is yours after you graduate from training," he added, interrupting the current conversation.

"Daddy, that's your favorite! I can't take it."

"Yes, you can. You take this magnificent tree with you, with all its magical powers, and you will always have me with you…"

▲

NOW

Hunter found Margaux in the conference room behind the cockpit, already changed into a pair of spandex jeans and a plain gray tank top, with white tennis shoes. She was strapped into a standard passenger seat and reading the mission brief on her tablet. Hunter stored her bag in her cabin and joined the Whisker.

"Hunter, may I ask a question?"

"Always," Hunter replied as she hunched over the conference table to read her reports on her own tablet.

"Why isn't this missing-persons case being handled by local authorities?"

The agent spoke softly but officially. "As rare as it occurs, when a Task Force employee goes missing, it's handled internally. We keep it out of the local authorities and other federal departments, because they have too many media connections, and we're supposed to stay under everyone's radar."

"I feel…" Margaux began, "…I feel like you're going to make a very important discovery soon."

"Oh? Just how did you suddenly decide that?"

Margaux politely smiled in reply. "That's The Way it works."

Hunter smiled. "I think you're going to be very interesting to work with on this trip…"

CHAPTER 3

WHISKER TWITCHINGS

The wait staff took away the lunch plates and silverware from the table in the plane's conference room. Hunter moved her tablet in front of her on the table and activated her own mission brief, and Margaux followed suit. The Whisker agent quickly noticed that their versions were not identical. "You have information on your tablet that I don't," she said.

"There was information I wanted to tell you alone after we were on the way," said Hunter, "and I was uncomfortable talking about it with other ears around."

"What about the plane's staff?"

"They know to stay out when I turn on the red light." Hunter waved her hand over the table surface, and a virtual interface flared to life in the reflective top. She moved her fingers above the table, making the interface images slide to the left until a keypad set appeared. She tapped several keys, and both agents heard the doors fore and aft click. "Now, we're secure and private. They can move front and back through the starboard walkway and leave us alone."

"Wow," said Margaux. "Zis is almost like in a movie!"

Hunter smiled. Margaux's youthful energy was a pleasant change of pace from that of her teammates, aside from Agent Proteus, the youngest field team member. No matter what the mission, Proteus always had an undying sense of fun and adventure. Margaux reminded her of Proteus.

"So," Margaux continued, "what is there to tell me that is not in the official report?"

Now you sound a lot like Mark, Hunter thought. "Well, you've read that we're off to find Professor Windimer. What I asked to have left out was, well…"

Margaux's innocent look was almost as overpowering as Mark's terrifying scowls.

"He was, well," Hunter continued, "on vacation in Washington State, on one of his eccentric, ah, hobbies." Margaux continued to look at her calmly. "He was apparently following up on new clues for—for—"

"For?" Margaux asked.

"Damn. Bigfoot! Sasquatch! Yeti! Whatever that fairy-tale monster is called in the American northwest."

The Cat Whisker didn't react. "Bigfoot or Sasquatch, ma'am. Yeti is the name for the Abominable Snowman in Nepal and Tibet."

Hunter looked at Margaux in disbelief and surprise. "Do you believe that kinda creature is real? Even though no one's ever captured one dead or alive, and those photographs and videos are at best always fuzzy and distant."

Margaux looked back innocently. "Do you believe in your native gods even though you've never seen one in person and none have ever been photographed?"

"How long were you standing in that doorway when Proteus and I were talking?"

"Sorry?"

"Never mind. I get your point, though. What I do is track down people. Seeker's the one who tracks down the exotic or ancient. It's just that, for all the supposed 'witnesses' and 'evidence', there's nothing that convinces me that an eight-foot-tall hairy humanoid exists. And Professor Windimer going off on one of his wild Bigfoot chases is not only unsettling but, frankly, asinine, as far as I'm concerned. Always have been."

The Whisker simply smiled at her. It suddenly seemed to Hunter like Margaux was looking through her before refocusing back on her eyes. "You will see the way, ma'am."

"What? What way?"

Margaux ignored her question and returned her attention to the mission brief. "So, after we land and unload, what's the plan, ma'am?"

Hunter looked at her curiously then returned to their conversation. "We'll check into a hotel for the night." She tabbed an icon on her tablet. "We have adjoining rooms waiting for us already. We'll get dinner and then a good night's rest. Then we'll take off first thing in the morning." She keyed another icon and showed the screen to her partner. "Proteus is still receiving the GPS ping from his phone, that's where we're heading."

"How does his phone battery still have power after, what, three or four days now?"

"All TF phones have a non-market long-life battery in them. Standard charge can last up to seven days in standby, even with the GPS on. Too expensive for commercial purchase yet. Jason Enterprises is still working on the product, trying to make them more, um, technologically advanced. One part of that is to give it an even longer battery life, using solar power and other techie stuff."

"Ah," said Margaux. "Oh, quick, grab your coffee cup, please."

"What?" Hunter asked, instinctively taking hold of her cup. The plane tipped and shook for a few seconds, hard enough that her cup would have dropped to the carpet. "How—?"

"You are welcome," said the Cat Whisker as she got up from the conference table and took a seat by a window.

"Sorry about the turbulence," the pilot said over the speakers. "Everyone okay back there?"

Hunter said aloud to the pilot's open speaker as she stared at Margaux, "Yeah, we're good." She blinked several times, baffled, and continued, "We're real good…"

CHAPTER 4

THE FIRST DISAPPEARANCE

Margaux returned to her seat with a steaming cup of coffee, sat, and picked up her tablet from the seat beside hers. The screen flared to life when she pressed her fingertip to its surface.

Hunter looked up from her tablet two seats over and said, "So, you've been studying the mission brief for a while now. You have any questions?"

Margaux looked up, set her tablet down on the seat, and sipped at her coffee. "Would you tell me about yourself? What is it that makes you The Hunter of Task Force?"

Hunter smiled and chuckled. "Why don't you use your mind-reading powers to tell you all about me?"

The Cat Whisker agent smiled back and sipped her coffee again. "I'm a sensitive, Hunter. Now there is a Whisker who has an exceptionally high ESPer rating—"

"You're kidding me, right? You actually have a mind-reader in your group?"

"You amaze me, Hunter. The open part of your Task Force file indicates that you've traveled across the world in search of fugitives or missing persons, survived dangers and traps that a layman might call borderline-paranormal, and yet you still think of us as freaks or liars."

"Everything I've seen in this job," said Hunter, "has been logically explained to my satisfaction. Well, except for one thing…"

Margaux eyebrows rose slightly. "And what is that?"

"Our leader, Agent Spy of the field team…he has this incredible talent of seemingly disappearing from one spot and reappearing somewhere else without anyone ever seeing him do either. He vanishes from tracking systems of every kind. It's like he's a ghost or something, sometimes."

Margaux tilted her head in contemplation, and then smiled as she replied, "Oh, Spy is very human. But he also possesses—" She stopped speaking; her brow furrowed gently.

"Possesses what?"

Margaux opened her mouth to say something, but stopped, then smiled before answering. "A secret he learned long ago when he was a Navy SEAL."

"Son of a bitch!" Hunter exclaimed, leaning forward as she slapped a hand on her armrest. "We'll never figure out how he does it."

"Is it really that important?" Margaux asked. "To know someone's secret?"

"Well," replied Hunter, sitting back in her seat. "No, it's not that important…some of us just hate a mystery, that's all…"

▲

TWO YEARS AGO

"I know you're married, but may I say just once and never again that you just look incredibly hot?" Mae-Lei asked as he blushed a deep red.

Mark Jason looked down at his well-muscled body in its new fitted Task Force uniform and gun belt. "You may this one time, because I think my wife will be the first one to agree with you very whole-heartedly." He smiled at her. "Our secret, I promise. So, where are we?"

She punched in a numeric code on the keypad next to the nondescript door in one of Task Force Divisions generic hallways. "Your predecessor and Tom Michelson designed this test after the first couple times a field agent was killed. Dozens of enemy combat simulations were developed to test new candidates for their reactions in the field after months of training. You, sir, are to go in without all the training, per Tom's orders. Said something about wanting to see what you can really do."

Mark smiled, his grin a bright contrast against the frame of his brown box beard. He slipped the black hood of his uniform over his head, attaching the few electronic wires to the collar seam before sealing the hood and collar together all the way around his neck. The black lenses in the eye holes hid his eyes completely. He pressed a flexible stud below his larynx and spoke, his voice now changed to a deep baritone. "Testing, testing. Very nice, I like the way this sounds. Now what?"

"Your test, sir, is to take out the five terrorists attempting to place a suitcase explosive in one of the buildings of this small neighborhood, retrieve the suitcase, and return to the launch site without injury." She handed him a .45 automatic. "Your bullets, and theirs, are all paint bullets. You bring back the suitcase intact, and no red stains on your brand-new suit."

He took the gun and placed it in its holster, leaving the security strap unhooked. She pressed the "enter" button and the pocket door slid into the wall. The room within was black. He was about to activate the sensors in his hood when she stopped his arm. "No using the electronics in this test, but you also have to get used to wearing the hood."

Hunter guided him five feet into the darkness, the light from the hallway the only illumination casting their shadows deep into the darkness. She pressed a button on the hand-control she held. The darkness lightened as the massive test area was lit to reveal a recreated typical rural neighborhood late at night. Some windows were illuminated, automatons moving behind curtains or open windows like real residents in the homes. A car pulled into a driveway; the driver got out and entered one of the houses. A dog barked somewhere unseen. "Your task begins…" She looked over at him, but he was already gone. "What the hell? Where'd you go?" She stepped back outside into the hall, but she was alone.

Hunter keyed the door closed and activated the test monitor on the wall. There were five circle icons on the screen, but a sixth one she should have seen was not there; a diamond shape that was to have represented Mark's position on the grid. "Where the hell are you, Mark?"

She ran a diagnostic on her screen to make sure his tracker was active, but the software reported back no signal. She involuntarily gasped as she saw a diamond icon flash to life beside one of the testing agents, then flash back off as that circle changed from white to red, indicating that enemy was "killed". In rapid progression his icon appeared four more times, and the remaining four circles changed from white to red; all his targets were "dead". The diamond flashed one more time on the opposite side of the door. Hunter keyed the open-sequence again and the door slid back open to the dark neighborhood but no Mark. She stepped to the door, her hands resting on both door frames. "Mark? Hello?"

"Mission accomplished," she heard behind her. She jumped as she spun on her heel, reaching for her gun...but it was no longer in her holster. Mark held her .357 in one hand and the target suitcase in the other.

"How the hell did you do that?" she demanded loudly.

He handed her weapon back, butt-first. "Just something I picked up along the way…"

▲

NOW

Margaux rose and moved to sit next to Hunter. "If I tell you something, will you answer my question?"

Hunter looked her in the eyes and saw a deep wisdom in eyes so young. "Sure. I think."

The Whisker stared back, smiling. "There will be someone who can see through his secret, and he will die but not die. And The Spy will be reborn." Her French accent was suddenly deep and accentuated.

Hunter stared at her. "What the hell was that, Chocolate?"

Margaux blinked innocently. "What was what?"

"You said something about The Spy dying but not dying."

"Indeed," she replied.

"You know why I have such trouble believing in what you do? Because you spit out gibberish like that and then act like you said nothing important or unusual." Hunter sat back again, returning to reading her mission brief.

"You really need to answer it."

"What, answer what?" Hunter asked. The phone in her pocket rang. "Stop doing that!" She looked at the number on her display; it was her mother's number. "Hi, Mother."

"Hello, Mae-Lei," said the pleasant female voice on the other end. "Just wanted to make sure you were on the way home for your birthday."

Hunter grinned, knowing she couldn't disclose her mission. "No, Mother, I'm actually working today."

"Working? Well, that's a shame, dear, we had things all planned out. Your father was looking forward to throwing you a big dinner for your thirty-fifth birthday. Why are you having to work? Why didn't you call and say something?"

"I'm sorry, Mother. We had a sudden, ah, loss of inventory in my department at work that has to be recovered. It wasn't negotiable, and honestly, I just forgot to call you. I'm sorry. Should only take a couple days or so if all goes well. Maybe I can head home after?"

"That would be wonderful! I'll tell Lani you're still coming home, just a few days late."

"Tell Lani to relax and have some tea, I look forward to seeing him, too. I'm sorry, Mother, but I have to go. I'll be home soon, okay?"

"Okay, Mae-Lei. Good luck, and we'll see you soon! We love you! Aloha!"

"Aloha, and I love you," said Hunter, ending the call and returning the phone to her pocket.

"Who is Lani?" Margaux asked.

Hunter looked at her for a moment, her emotional shields suddenly flaring up in defense, but realized it wasn't necessary. She relaxed herself internally and replied, "Lani was my boyfriend in high school. He was as godlike as Kamehameha to the girls in high school, he wanted to marry me and settle down, but I wanted to go into the army and see the world while he was content to stay in Hilo."

"And?"

"And then," Hunter said with a sigh, "the opportunity to join the Task Force was dropped in my lap." She tucked her long legs up under herself in her chair, feeling unusually content in talking about herself to a perfect stranger. "I was told I'd made a name for myself in Afghanistan and Iraq as an army tracker, finding and capturing or killing the hiding al-Qaida terrorists. I'd just finished my second tour when I was transferred to Washington, not knowing why. I was just waiting around and finally Colonel Michelson called me in and made an offer I couldn't refuse. The rest, as the saying goes, is history..."

▲

FIVE YEARS AGO

Army Captain Mae-Lei Komala set her father's bonsai tree in its place of honor in the corner of her apartment living room, surrounded by small Hawaiian sculptures and votive candles. "Well, Dad," she said to the tree, "this was the second move in three months for me, and I'm not exactly sure why. I wasn't even given who I'm supposed to report to, just to move here to Fairfax and into this apartment already leased for me...a long-term lease, too, and already paid for!" She noticed a brown leaf on the tree, picked up a small plant clipper, and gently cut off the dead stem. "Even worse, I was ordered not to talk about this transfer to anyone, not my old CO, no one. My orders are to wait until contacted." She lightly sprayed some water on the tree, then sat on her light tan couch. "So, what is there to do in Fairfax?"

Mae-Lei had been sitting on her couch long enough to kick off her shoes and stretch out on the couch while she watched an old episode of Hawaii Five-O on the TV. "Jack Lord was SO hot!" she said aloud. "God, I miss home sometimes..."

She jumped when she heard a knock on the door. Instinctively she grabbed for one of the automatics she had hidden throughout her apartment as she tiptoed toward the door. Halfway to the door she stopped and shook her head. "I'm in a friggin' apartment in a city. Who the hell could be a threat here?" She stuck the gun in the back of her waistband and continued to the door and looked out the peephole. She saw two men in black suits, white shirts, and black glasses. "Yes?" she asked through the door.

"Captain Komala?" one of them said. "You are expecting us."

She opened her door as far as the chain would allow. "Who are you?"

"We're from Task Force Division, with the offer of a lifetime for you." One of them extended his hand toward the narrow opening. "My name is Marshall Gray, Captain, and I'm inviting you to come help us keep the world safe..."

▲

NOW

"Not quite," Margaux said sympathetically.

Hunter was taken aback. How does she know? Aw, what the hell. "I went through my months of training and was finally assigned as The Hunter for the field team, replacing the prior Agent Hunter, who was killed in action. It was great, in the beginning. I mean, after all, I had access to the most incredible weapons, and got to travel around the world with the team or on my own, even started collecting specimens of weapons from all different cultures. Then, there was one mission where the previous Agent Spy and I were assigned to infiltrate an organization as, well, a married couple…and, yeah, we sort of fell in love." Hunter looked past Margaux and out the cabin window at the clear skies scattered with white clouds, and the distant earth below. She remembered a similar flight a few years earlier, when she and Marshall Gray, the first Spy of Task Force, were returning from one particular mission where they posed as husband and wife…and even joined the Mile High Club together. She could still recall the taste of his lips, his skin, and the way he felt when he held her in his arms. She blinked several times and took a sip from her coffee before she continued. "The love we pretended to make became very real love…and it was incredible. Every time was better than the last, and he was ready to retire and marry me. Then," Hunter lowered her head; tears welled in her eyes. "He was murdered on assignment…"

▲

TWO YEARS AGO

Mae-Lei turned the corner of the Jefferson Davis Arts Center in Richmond, Virginia, as she followed the sound of two gunshots in the night. She looked down and found a Task Force gun belt pouch on the ground; it contained sonic grenades and one was missing.

She retrieved the pouch with her gloved fingers and examined it. She saw through her own polarized lenses one of the four small sonic grenades was missing. She wedged the pouch under the metal buckle of her gun belt, as there was no room to add the abandoned pouch on her own and peered around the corner cautiously.

She saw a black body lying on the ground halfway to the garden shed, and plenty of blood on the ground. A rush of adrenalin flowed through her body, and she felt her heartbeat pounding in her ears. Looking around the area quickly, detecting no movement and hearing nothing, and no heat signatures visible in her glasses, she determined the area was safe, and approached carefully.

Spy lay in the grass, the bullet hole in the left sunglass lens answered her unasked question, and a closer look revealed a trail of blood flowed down his left cheek and temple. There was no movement in his chest, no respiration. She quickly took stock of the immediate area. His holster was empty, and his pistol was nowhere to be found, although she saw a .44 Magnum discarded nearby. Protruding out from under his blood-smeared buckle was a folded piece of paper. She carefully removed it and unfolded it. It looked like a Bible verse. When she spoke, the comm unit in her ear activated, and she said softly but firmly, "Command, this is

Hunter. 10-100, agent down. Request cleaning crew and containment ASAP. Lock onto my phone's GPS." She ended the call and holstered her pistol, fighting to hold her emotions in check.

Hunter looked at the note again, trying to make sense of the strange message, then looked up and stared into the stars. She allowed one tear to fall as she knelt by her friend, then another, and more, until she cried openly while she was alone with him, holding his left hand in both of hers.

▲

NOW

"And you've been alone ever since?"

"Yeah." Hunter stabbed a finger on the comm button on her armrest. "Hey, would someone get some whiskey in here on the double, please? Seems we're in great need!" She released the button and waited for one of the wait staff to hurry in with a bottle and two glasses. He left just as quickly. Hunter poured a doubler shot into her tumbler and took a deep swig of whiskey. "Okay, I enjoyed that, I admit it. So, where was I?" She refilled her tumbler full and took a deep sip. "Alone. Yeah. The new Spy, the current one, had such a creative way of catching my Spy's murderer and stopping him in a way that Mars…my Spy…would have definitely approved. I finally got to say goodbye to him, but just haven't felt the need or desire to look for anyone else…until my Mother just mentioned Lani. Actually, I wonder why now?"

"I get the feeling it's because of this mission."

Hunter looked at her quizzically. "How do you mean?"

Margaux stepped to the counter on the wall to pour a glass of water. "The way you so adamantly dismiss Professor Windimer's belief in the Sasquatch, it was more than just a scientific disbelief…I sensed a great deal of emotional attachment. You had a relationship with him."

"I'm so gonna freekin' shoot Spy," Hunter murmured. "Yeah, you're right again. Harold came between Lani and my fiancé between the years. And I've never forgotten Harold, either. And that's why I was picked for this mission, too, because I have a personal attachment and incentive to find him."

"So, after you find him, what will you do then?"

"What do you mean, what will I do? I guess go home for a late birthday celebration then return to work." Hunter finished her tumbler. Hunter decided to change the subject. "Okay, enough of me. What's your department actually about? And why in the hell are you called 'Cat Whiskers'?"

Margaux smiled in pride. "Cats can navigate at night with almost no light, relying on their night vision and sensory input from the whiskers, hence our name. As for what we do, we guide or advise by means outside technology, basically. We have members who have the same talent I do, which is sensing what is around us to determine in advance of an action. We have ESPers, who can read minds or thoughts, mentalists who can read emotions more accurately than lie detectors, telekinetic people who can move objects with only their thoughts, and so on. How many times in your life, or in your work, have you had a feeling about something? Perhaps something was going to happen or that someone was watching you? As a hunter you rely upon heightened senses as second nature. You accept these abilities as part of you, without question. Again, a cat can walk through a completely dark space and avoid any obstacle partly because the whiskers are sensitive to things such as the movement of air or the change in electrical fields."

"Yes, but those are trained and taught abilities. These claims of you being born with extra-sensory abilities are a bit of a reach, even today. Too close to X-Men kinda stuff, or whatever."

Margaux got to her feet and gently paced the conference room. "With all the metal detectors and body scanners around now, if you wanted to kill someone without a single weapon—wouldn't it be great to have someone who could take someone's pen out of his pocket and turn it into a bullet without even touching it? No one to blame, because most people would never consider the possibility of someone with voodoo powers having done it…that's not the correct wording, but you know what I mean. We must pay attention to the sixth, seventh, and eight senses we all have, but only a few have realized, and fewer still have utilized." She raised her arms and wiggled her fingers like a stage magician.

"So, you're all being trained as assassins?"

"Of course not. I was just giving you an extreme example. But if trained properly, can't a Cat Whisker be as useful on a mission as I hope to be with you this time?"

Hunter stretched out her legs in her seat. "Well, Chocolate", Hunter said, "you've made for an interesting conversationalist. I honestly look forward to seeing how you handle yourself in the field tomorrow." She saw another distant look in the Whisker's eyes. "Whaaaat? What now?"

"Beware the red. Follow the red. Ignore, be dead."

Hunter shook her head. "You are very odd, agent Whisker."

"Thank you, ma'am…"

CHAPTER 5

SETTLING

The Task Force transport landed uneventfully at Joint Base Lewis-McChord. The safari vehicle was unloaded from the belly, and Hunter drove Margaux and herself to a nearby hotel where they had rooms already reserved. It was a pair of adjoining rooms with a connecting door.

The safari vehicle was outfitted with biometric scanners made for: locking, unlocking, accessing, starting the vehicle, even restraints holding the weapons and equipment in the rear.

After both women were settled in their rooms, Hunter knocked on the connecting door to Margaux. "You busy?" she asked.

The Whisker agent replied, "Not at all, come in, please." Margaux was sitting on her bed in a meditative posture. "I'm trying to open my senses to this locale, it's very strange to me."

"How so?"

"This is a new place for me, I must try to become one with the locale in order to be of help to you."

"Well, while you are becoming one with the Seattle area, take a look at this and tell me if I have what I need to be a...Bigfoot hunter." She handed her tablet over to Margaux.

"Why? You're not hunting for Bigfoot; you're hunting for Professor Windimer."

"True, but I figure in this case the fastest way to find him is to follow the signs he would follow."

Margaux nodded in approval. "That makes perfect sense." She took the tablet and read through some of the evidence gathered by various Sasquatch hunting groups and organizations on their websites. "Very thorough list. I have no doubt you'll be able to find the way easily enough."

Hunter sat on the foot of the bed, facing her. "You keep saying 'the way'. What way?"

Margaux smiled, in satisfaction. "Yes, you will see the way."

Hunter rolled her eyes.

Margaux closed her eyes and returned to her meditation. Hunter rose gently, picking up her tablet as she did, and returned to her room, closing the door quietly behind her. "That girl is 'way' out there..."

▲

The next morning both women were dressed in matching hunter green uniforms, dark green knee-high leather boots, and elbow-high dark green leather gloves. When they approached the safari, Hunter held her right palm up over the door panel, which immediately unlocked when it recognized her physiology. Margaux did the same on the passenger side.

Hunter reached behind the driver's seat and withdrew her standard black-leather Task Force gun belt, a Glock attached to the holster slat by biometric-reader steel clips, black leather equipment pouches attached the entire length of the belt, and the buckle was a flat non-reflective metal with an equilateral triangle etched in the metal, the symbol of the Hunter agent for the Task Force field team.

She then reached back again and removed a second weapon, a .50 caliber rifle, and handed it to Margaux. "I read you were a good shot with this," Hunter said, "so familiarize yourself with it and your pouch contents. I loaded them based on what I anticipate us needing on this mission."

"Thank you, ma'am," said the French woman. As her hand grasped the belt by the gun slat, the retaining pins clicked, and the gun came free in her hand as the belt itself fell to the ground.

"The sensors have already been programmed with your physiology," said Hunter, "and the gun is also programmed to only be fired by you, no one else. And the same goes for all your equipment."

"C'est bonne," Margaux replied. She reattached the Glock to the slat, fastened the belt around her waist, and got in the passenger's seat.

Hunter got in the driver's seat and first activated the GPS tracker on the computerized dashboard. "This is already preset with the professor's phone signal. That's where we go first." She pressed a communication button on the dashboard. "Tactical, this is Hunter."

"Tactical, tied in, Hunter," said a male voice over the speakers.

"Please advise all local authorities that I will be exceeding all speed limits and to ignore our vehicle. Will be leaving Tacoma and heading north on highway 16, then highway 3."

There was some keyboard clicking sounds on the speakers before the aide at Task Force Division in Washington D.C. said, "Authorities have been notified, Hunter. You are clear to go at your desired speed."

"Thank you, Tactical." She turned to Margaux and smiled. "Off we go."

"Ready," said Margaux.

Minutes later they were headed north on state highway 16, and as a courtesy to the local highway patrol she turned on the blue flashing lights in the bumper as the safari traveled at speeds approaching 100 miles per hour.

"So," Hunter began after they were a few miles on the road, "what did you do to impress Agent Spy enough to specifically recommend you being on this mission?"

"I went home for a drink..."

▲

TWELVE YEARS AGO

Mark Jason was just finishing his first year on the job as president of the family business, Jason Enterprises, following the transition training from his father, Zachary. While Mark was a known entity from all the years he'd spent visiting the company as a youth and then as a naval officer, there were some within the company who didn't feel it fair that the young son should take over right out of the navy when others had worked there for years and would never take over. "While this company is still a family business," Zachary growled from his wheelchair at one complaining employee, "the family runs it. If you don't like it, you're welcome to quit and find someone else who'll pay you the kinda salary I'm paying you." Those few learned to shut up quickly, as Zachary was an indomitable force even in his final months at the company before cancer took his life, and everyone soon realized that Mark was not only a more demanding leader than Zachary but also more compassionate to employees' needs. Mark also demonstrated quickly that he knew much more about the company than most of its employees.

After his first year as company president, no one questioned when Mark assigned his wife Jan to the new position of executive vice-president.

Also, at the end of his first year, the company set a record percentage gross profit, and every employee received the largest annual company profit share bonus in the company's history.

Zachary performed the last company budget while Mark was still settling in the president's office on the twentieth floor, but now it was Mark's turn. Jan had a much better set of financial skills than Mark and so it was that she worked with the accounting department to prepare the next fiscal year's budget.

She entered Mark's office, where he was discussing his day's schedule with his assistant Lisa. "Good morning, Lisa," said Jan, her long bright red hair flowing around her shoulders like a silk curtain.

"Good morning, Mrs. Jason," said the middle-aged woman. Lisa had been Zachary's assistant since the day Zachary started the company and had watched Mark grow up from the scrawny boy into the well-muscled man he was today. "You're looking beautiful as always, ma'am."

Jan smiled and blushed. "Please, Lisa, I keep telling you to call me 'Jan'. And you look magnificent yourself."

Lisa smiled back. "Thank you, ma'am… Jan. I have lost a few pounds recently." She lifted her arms and did a gentle model's pose in the chair. Lisa had indeed lost weight from her 200+ pound figure.

"Congratulations!" Jan replied as she bent over to give a gentle hug. "But you shouldn't worry about a few pounds, you're gorgeous as you are. Speaking of appearances, though," she said as she rounded Mark's desk and scratched her fingernails on Mark's stubbly face, "this man insists on growing a beard." She put her hands on Mark's ears. "Don't let him hear, but I really think it's sexy. Only thing is I don't know what kinda beard shape to let him grow." She released his ears and he looked up at her in a teasing scowl.

"My daddy, God rest his soul, had the most beautiful full beard I ever saw on a man," Lisa said proudly. She looked at Mark. "Sincerely, sir, a full beard on you would look good, too, but keep it trimmed close. A statuesque man like you should have the beard of a Roman God, if I may say."

Mark laughed. "I've been called a lot of things, but, my dear, that was a first!"

"So, how about we do a Roman theme for the next company picnic?" Jan asked.

"You, my love, will dress as Athena."

"Who may I come as?" Lisa asked. "I do plan to go off my diet and enjoy myself!"

"Edesia," said Mark. "She was the goddess of food at the feast. And may all the employees worship you as the goddess you are!"

They all enjoyed a long laugh. Finally, Jan said, "Well, I hate to bring up business at work, but there's a problem with the budget."

"Problems are not allowed," said Mark seriously. "Whatcha got?"

"There's an off-budget allocation from Zachary's budget last year, but there's no notation on what it was for. Lisa?" She handed the report to Lisa. "What's that fiscal code for? There's no corresponding code in the financials."

"I don't know," Lisa admitted, "at least, I don't know the department but I recognize part of the code as one Zachary used for his top-secret stuff. I'd tell you where to look it up, but you can't access it."

"Why not?" Mark asked.

"Because he kept that in his head, God rest his soul."

Mark sat back in his executive chair. "Well, there's only one way to find out what it is. Jan, cut it from the budget but leave the money unappropriated. Let's find out who has a cow about it."

TWO MONTHS LATER…

Lisa stepped into Mark's office. "There's a Miss Martell to see you, Mr. Jason."

Mark looked up from his reports, his unasked question of "Who is Miss Martell?" clear on his face but without insulting his unknown guest. Lisa's gentle nod told him that he was about to meet the unknown budget money receiver. "Send her in, please, Lisa," he said as he closed his folio.

A petite brunette who wore her hair in a ponytail entered the office, and Lisa left, closing the connecting door behind her. Mark rose and extended his hand in greeting. "Miss Martell, a pleasure to meet you."

"Mrs.," she corrected. "Mrs. Desiree Martell, Cat Whisker Division."

"Cat what? Cat what! Are we making pet food somewhere in this building or something?"

"You don't know about that, do you, sir?" she asked calmly.

"Well, it does appear you have me at an incredibly severe disadvantage, Mrs. Martell. Please, sit, and enlighten me." He motioned at one of the chairs opposite his desk. "Would you like something to drink?"

Desiree sat and crossed her legs at the knees. "Thank you, but no." Her eyes fell on the gold key on its wooden block, Zachary Jason's symbol of the company president. "Your father created the Cat Whisker Division, Mr. Jason."

"I've already gathered that much, thank you, that's why I had to take the action of temporarily stopping your budget to find out what Dad was up to. But what exactly is the Cat Whisker Division?"

"It is," she said proudly, "the department that doesn't exist."

THIRTY MINUTES LATER

"Your father was always interested in the paranormal," Desiree said.

"Yes, I know," Mark agreed.

"So he wanted to finance the most serious testing of people who could do more outside the five standard senses. He called us the Cat Whiskers because we exhibited traits like felines: heightened senses and reactions, greater awareness of our surroundings, precognition, telekinesis. On the official Jason Enterprises flowchart, we are 'off-budget expenditures', but we are regularly dispatched to help the police on some of the more, shall I say, 'exotic' cases. Would you mind taking a trip in your elevator?"

Intrigued, Mark replied, "Sure." They both rose and walked through Lisa's office to the executive elevator used only by Mark and Jan.

The private elevator car that ran direct from Mark's office level to the Jason family's private parking area came to a stop as always at the ground level. Desiree placed her palm against the flat metal screen, which suddenly glowed under her hand. A virtual keypad appeared on the metal, and she pressed the "5" button.

"What the hell is that?" he asked.

"Zachary built in special overrides for all Cat Whiskers. We come in like any other employee, and the elevators are programmed with our genetic markers which produce the buttons so we can go to our 'offices'. We need peace and quiet and isolation from the rest of the company so we can do our work."

"Which is?"

"Help people, of course, Mister Jason."

The elevator floor light showed the below-ground floors. It reached the last level, SB5, and came to a stop. Before the doors parted Desiree inserted a key into the fire department override and turned it counterclockwise... and the elevator resumed its downward motion to SB6. "There's another level?" Mark asked in astonishment.

The doors parted when the car came to a stop. A young girl was standing outside the door. "You made it!" she squealed happily as she ran into the car... and wrapped her arms around Mark's legs.

"And who is this?" Mark asked.

He noted the surprised look on Desiree's face. "This is my daughter, Margaux." She stared in shock at her daughter holding onto her boss so tightly, and then a smile formed on her face.

"Care to share the joke?" Mark asked cheerfully.

"Not a joke, Mister Jason," Desiree said as she reached into her pocket. She pulled out a folded piece of paper that had been taped together with a familiar circular stamp on it. "I had this notarized at the Post Office the day she wrote this," she said, "as proof that it is real."

Mark took the taped paper from her and looked at the post office's cancellation stamp date. "Hm, interesting… I was in China then, taking some… classes…"

"Margaux doesn't say a word or make a sound around here, but she has been tested as near-genius level on all aptitude tests. But, like the rest of us here, she has special... talents, sir." She handed him the paper. "She told me years ago, that is, she wrote to me that I would know who to give this to, and when."

He took the taped folded paper and knelt to Margaux's level. "Is this for me?" he asked gently.

"Yes, sir," Margaux replied in a flawless French-accented English dialect.

Desiree gasped. She had never heard her daughter speak before this.

Mark looked up at Desiree, then back to Margaux. "Am I to open this now?"

Margaux nodded happily. He smiled and gently peeled back the tape, sealed and stamped for over six years. He unfolded the paper and read the hand-written poem:

"The doors will part

To the man in black.

When his heart is black

Is when I will save his heart."

Mark looked down at his gray suit. "I'm afraid you guessed the color wrong, young lady."

"Not yet," Margaux said, smiling...

DECEMBER 2011

The Recovery Room Bar was a popular meeting place for the retired and former military in the Richmond, Virginia area to gather for drinks and food to reminisce and celebrate their service and friends lost. The owner was known only as Al to all the patrons, and the wait staff were all beautiful young women who wore tight patriotic-colored shirts and pants.

Mark Jason sat at the bar alone, his cousin TJ, the bar's bouncer and head waitress, refilling his drink. "You okay, cous?" she asked.

"Yeah," he said coldly to her. "Just fantastic."

"You don't sound it."

"Not in the mood, cous."

"You and my raging hot cousin-in-law have a fight?" TJ asked.

"No," he said as he took a deep drink. "But there was a fight."

TJ lightly tapped the bar with her fingernails, getting Al's attention. The curvaceous brunette stepped away while the rotund mustachioed owner took her place. "You wanna talk, Mark?" he asked gently.

"Not really."

Al leaned close. "Have anything to do with this Biblical Bomber case that's been in the papers again?"

Mark looked at him, tired eyes asking a silent question: "How?"

"Look, I know you. And I know you took out that terrorist as part of your secret little group." Mark looked at him quizzically. "Don't ask how, your level isn't high enough yet. All the people you've killed across the world as a SEAL probably didn't prepare you for having to kill someone so young as The Bomber. But you did what you were supposed to, and God knows that. Lives were saved because of you."

Mark silently lifted his drink at Al in salute.

The bar door opened, and a petite young woman entered and took the seat next to Mark at the bar, placing her clutch on the surface. She said softly, "Cognac, please." As Al fixed her drink she said to Mark, "Bon soir, monsieur."

"Good evening," he replied.

Al set her order before her and stepped away.

"To life," she toasted.

Mark looked at her for a moment.

She took a silent sip and set her glass down. She opened her clutch and took out a folded piece of paper, taped closed, a red circular stamp on the tape, and handed it to Mark. Familiar handwriting under the tape read: "The Man in Black".

He looked at her, eyes wide in sudden recognition. "Margaux?"

She smiled gently and placed a small hand on his forearm. "Embrace the darkness. Let it empower you. Use the darkness to save the light."

His eyes narrowed in recognition. "Margaux, what's a Cat Whisker like you doing in a gin joint like this?"

"Looking for a job. Do you have any openings in the Cat Whisker Division?"

"I didn't know you were gone. So anyway, why would you want to come back after all these years?" he asked.

"Because it was time, mon frere. I sensed your disturbance and came home."

His eyes narrowed when she called him "her brother". "Came home from where?"

She smiled. "From where I was." She took another sip. "You're not the only one who knows how to come and go unseen always at the right time ..."

THIRTEEN MONTHS AGO

Margaux sat alone on a bench at Fountain Lake Park. As always, the water was smooth when the fountain in its center was turned off. The late autumn air had a slight chill to it, not uncomfortable, and she was very comfortable in her one-piece dress and cardigan.

She was surrounded by a circle of yellow police tape. Three feet in front of her was the white tape outline of a human form. A woman was found raped and dead there earlier in the day, according to the police reports. The Cat Whisker Division was asked to help when forensics found absolutely nothing to aid in determining who did it.

She closed her eyes and breathed in deeply and exhaled slowly, allowing her mind to relax and her senses to heighten. She was very adept at reading the world around her, as all actions by all creatures left energy signatures in their wakes. But in a well-visited locale as this in the Richmond suburbs, it was going to take her some time to filter out all the extraneous "noise".

She sat silently and unmoving for nearly an hour until she opened her eyes and rose to her feet. She slid off her flat shoes and walked barefoot into the center of the human-form tape outline. The energy of the victim's last few moments flowed within her and she turned to face the ground to her left where the road surrounding the lake curved to the right.

Margaux "saw" the assailant, and her last few seconds of life: he was wearing a brown jacket, darker brown pants. He smelled of alcohol, bourbon. Dark hair, black. He was pulling up his pants as he walked away next to the lake's edge. Something fell out of his pocket and into the water... something flat, shiny?

Margaux closed her eyes and stepped forward on her toes toward that spot in her vision, every movement gave a gentle electric surge in each toe. She came to a stop at the water's edge and looked down. A silver disc glistened just under the water. She stepped in the water to ankle depth, making the floating ducks quickly paddle away.

Margaux put on a pair of blue latex gloves, then knelt and reached for the disc. Her fingers gently touched it by the edge and picked it up from the submerged dirt.

"Thanks for finding it, babe," said a male voice from the benches.

Margaux looked up calmly. *It's him.*

"I'll take that if you don't mind," he demanded as he extended one hand while pointing a revolver at her with the other.

"Why did you kill her, Councilman?" Margaux asked calmly.

"It was an accident!" he countered angrily. "I hadn't had a drink in a year, and she insisted we have a drink after the fund-raiser. I didn't want to, but she smelled so good... and the bourbon was so tasty... and she kissed me..." His eyes began to tear. "It was an accident, but my wife can't know about it! I lost my AA 12-month badge after we had sex... after she threatened to blackmail me. Said she recorded us on her phone having sex here. I—I barely remember choking her in anger, and getting dressed..."

"Why didn't you just erase the recording from her phone?" she asked.

"Oh, come on, deleted files are never permanently deleted! Don't you watch the crime shows? So I threw her phone as far into the lake as I could, no one would think to look there." He lifted his gun hand higher. "I'm sorry, but you know everything now, I can't let you live. I'll take my badge first."

Margaux simply smiled as she removed a plastic bag from her cardigan pocket and dropped the disc in it.

"I said give it back! I'll shoot you; I swear!"

Margaux smiled bigger. "I don't think so."

Suddenly a black-clad arm reached around from behind him and took the gun from his hand. The Councilman spun around to stare at a man dressed in solid black from head to toe. He saw a gloved fist rear back and rocket toward his face... then nothing.

Margaux watched calmly as Spy dropped the murderer to the ground with one punch. She removed the surveillance bug from her pocket and turned it off. "If your father could see you now, he would be so incredibly proud. His son is a hero beyond all expectations. Not that I'm not grateful, but why exactly are you here? Not to save me."

The special electronics in his head mask made his voice a deep baritone. "I was actually on another case when I saw this scene unfolding. Figured you could use a friend."

She flexed her wrist and a Derringer dropped from its forearm spring-load assembly into her hand. "I wasn't in any danger."

He nodded gently. "Apparently I keep underestimating you."

They both heard sirens. "I imagine the police are on the way to arrest him, so you need to go back into the shadows before you're seen." She stepped out of the water and approached him. "I feel an incredible greatness in you, Mark Jason, and an even more incredible power. You have much good to do in the days to come... and whenever you ever need me, just say the word." As he turned to leave she said, "Your heart is red, for now. Be careful."

He nodded once. She nodded back and closed her eyes for only a moment... more than enough time for him to disappear into the twilight...

YESTERDAY

Margaux sat in her office in the Cat Whisker Division of Jason Enterprises. She had become a major consultant for the Richmond Police Department, to the point where she was constantly loaned out to departments across Virginia. She had been taking new Cat Whisker interns with her to teach them how to use their talents quietly to aid in murder investigations.

She was studying one case file intently when she felt her eyes cloud over, and she slowly placed the open file on her desk. Her head turned toward the phone, and her hand went to the cradle and gently grasped it. She remained frozen in pose for over two minutes until the phone rang. Margaux lifted the phone to her ear and said gently, "I've been expecting your call, Mister Jason."

"Of course, you have, Margaux," said her boss. "The word is given. I am texting you an address. Leave now." The line disconnected from his end, and she placed the cradle back down.

She rose from her desk and went to her office locker, removing a backpack and hanging suit bag; Mark had given her the bag with instruction to never open it until he gave the word. She opened it. She was not surprised to see three matching uniforms within: navy blue, hunter green, and white. At the bottom of the bag were three pairs each of matching leather boots and gloves.

She closed the bag; she would change into the blue uniform when she reached the secret Washington location of the Task Force Division. She slung her backpack over one shoulder and carried the suit back over the other arm.

Margaux closed and locked her office door, then headed for the elevator at the end of the hall. She stopped at the halfway point in front of a United States map. She turned her head and looked, not resisting the sudden urge to move her eyes up to the top left… at Washington state.

"The way…"

▲

NOW

An hour and a half later they arrived at Lake Crescent in Olympic National Forest. "His GPS trail leads past Lake Crescent Lodge," Hunter said, "and up into the trees. Sense anything yet, Whisker?"

"No, ma'am. I can't get a feel for anything when we're traveling this fast."

Hunter smiled and slowed the safari as she drove past the lodge along the lake's edge...

CHAPTER 6

AMBUSHED

Hunter guided the vehicle through the trees, easily following the undisturbed days-old trail of Harold Windimer's own vehicle. She drove over the top of a hill and observed an ATV stopped in the trees. She parked next to it and raised her Glock as she got out; she was cautious of everything around her, and slightly worried about Margaux's lack of experience in the field.

There were no occupants in the other vehicle, and the contents of the ATV seemed to be undisturbed. Hunter quietly opened a door to the vehicle, looked throughout but found no identifying papers. She scanned the vehicle plate numbers with her Task Force satellite computer phone and uploaded the number to her support staff at Task Force Division. "Tactical, I just sent you a vehicle number. I need owner information yesterday," she said quietly, still surveying her surroundings.

"Hunter, Tactical. Received scan, expediting response," replied a male voice from the speaker. Moments later he announced, "The vehicle is registered to Executive Terrain Vehicles, and leased to Harold Windimer."

"Copy, Tactical." She looked at Margaux. "Okay, Agent Chocolate, time to start earning your money. What do your senses tell you?"

"My common sense tells me you were too brave to open that door, not to mention damn suicidal. It could have been booby trapped. But I've been concentrating on the area the entire time."

Margaux returned her pistol to its clip holster and gently strode several feet away from the vehicles and Hunter. She closed her eyes, standing amongst the trees, breathing slow and deep, calming her body and opening her mind.

Her acuity of her senses increased...

...the buzzing of insects sounded like a brass band...

...coyote calls like operatic solos...

...elk munching on vegetation evoked a symphony of snare drums...

...a shuffle...

Margaux opened her eyes and turned to Hunter. "We are not alone, Hunter."

Hunter had misgivings about Margaux's words, but crouched into a defensive posture, nevertheless. "Where?"

The Whisker smiled. "We are not in any danger." She returned to Hunter's side. "Yet."

"Is there a threat to us? Or to Harold?" Hunter asked in a whisper.

"I cannot say," said Margaux. "Although I am certain the professor still lives."

Hunter studied the GPS tracker on her satellite phone. "His phone reads about half a mile west." A glance in that direction told her the path would be on foot. "We're hoofing it, Chocolate. Gear up." Hunter pulled a pack from behind her seat and slung it over her shoulders, attaching the mounting strips to her uniform top and sides. She donned her cocoon glasses and activated the embedded computer system within. The sensors began displaying readings of the environment around her, giving her an instant assessment of her surroundings. Elevation scans revealed distinctive human footwear impressions leading away from the ATV. "I have a path for us to follow, but it's straight uphill. Get your lungs ready for some huffing and puffing."

Margaux attached her pack to her back similarly. She smiled and whispered to herself, "We are on the way…"

Gunshots abruptly rang out and bullets bounced off the bulletproof Task Force safari and embedded into Harold's rental ATV…

CHAPTER 7

A CONVINCING CONVERSATION

"You know, you could have said something about sensing an ambush!" Hunter growled amid the explosions of gunshots on metal and wood, both diving to take cover behind the ATV.

"It doesn't exactly work that way," Margaux said calmly over the gunfire. "I am open for directions on how to get out of this!"

Hunter removed a scanner from her gun belt and activated it. The device displayed the heat signals of two figures approximately thirty yards away. She peered around the corner of their safari and noted where the shots originated, then sat back and removed another pouch from her belt. The pouch contained four metal cylinders with smaller metal extensions on one end; she removed two. From another pouch she removed two pieces of an air-powered pistol-like gun, connected them, and placed one of the cylinders in the barrel. Connecting the scanner readings to her glasses' software, she could precisely aim at their attackers without having to guess. She turned her body to face their direction, her glasses providing accurate distance as well as wind speed. She timed her return attack to a moment when the incoming fire paused.

Hunter rose, aimed, fired…reloaded the second cylinder in the barrel, changed angle, aimed, fired, and dropped, all within two seconds.

Two larger explosions echoed through the trees, followed by silence.

Hunter's glasses still displayed two heat signatures in the distant trees. "Stay here," she ordered Margaux. She dropped her small pistol and the pouches on the ground, removed the Glock from its holster clips, and carefully advanced on their attackers' location. When there was no resumption of gunfire she moved rapidly from tree to tree until she reached them.

On the ground lay two unconscious men twenty feet apart, with blood flowing from their ears and nostrils. One was holding an AK47 in his right hand; the other's rifle was several feet away. Even though both men were physically larger than she, Hunter had no trouble dragging them to separate trees and zip-tying them around the trunks. One of them she gagged, the other she slapped with her gloved hand to wake him up. "Hey, handsome," she said, as his eyes opened, "you wanna tell me why you're making Swiss cheese out of a perfectly good ATV?"

He opened his eyes and sneered at her. "I ain't tellin' you shit, bitch."

He never saw the green leather fist that suddenly gave him a broken nose. "Care to try that again, handsome?"

"Screw you!" he yelled, and spat blood from his mouth at her, but missed.

The pain in his face suddenly increased from a second punch, feeling his left cheekbone shatter. "You've got plenty of bones, handsome, and I've got all day. But before I start on your hands, I'm gonna make sure no woman wants to look at your face again."

"Alright, dammit!" he said in pain. "We're just paid to patrol this area and keep people out."

"Why?"

"I don't freekin' know or care! I sure as hell ain't paid enough to take on a Jungle Jane."

She pointed back toward the ATV's, "Where's the guy who was driving that ATV?"

"I don't know what you're talkin' about."

Instantly his other cheekbone cracked.

"Quit already, shit! I'm tellin' the damned truth! It was already abandoned when we found it! We left it alone 'cause our total orders when we got here were to keep people out and touch nothin'!"

Hunter stood and removed an item from a pouch at the back of her belt. It was a syringe loaded with a tranquilizer. The man watched in horror as she stabbed it into his carotid artery. His head fell forward, dropping into unconsciousness. She placed a gag over his mouth, then stepped to his still-unconscious partner and similarly injected him.

She turned to return to her partner, startled that she was only a few feet behind her. "Amazing," said Margaux, "you did all that without one increase in negative emotions."

"One doesn't become a Task Force agent if one panics under fire, or after having been under fire." She returned her syringe to its home on her belt. "You did pretty good over there by the way, Chocolate."

Margaux nodded in acknowledgement.

Hunter's brow furrowed for a moment, then turned back to her captives. She noticed both had walkie-talkies on their belts. "Shit. Chances are whoever hired these apes probably knows we're here." She jogged back to the safari and removed her compound bow and quiver of arrows. The quiver she attached to her backpack on one side and the bow on the other. She restored her weapon and concussion grenades to her belt from where she had left them on the ground. "Well, there's definitely something else going on beyond just a simple missing person," Hunter said. "Why else would there be armed guards in the middle of the forest?" She turned to Margaux. "OK, Whisker, I'll give you a point for noting that we weren't alone, so you do have some kinda good perception. What else can you tell me now?"

"We are alone, for now," Margaux replied. "You three created quite the ruckus."

"You know, for a little French woman you do have a good knowledge of American slang."

"I like Bruce Willis movies."

"Yippe-kay-yay. Let's go, Chocolate, we gotta move a lot faster now."

"Which way?"

"You don't sense 'the way'?"

Margaux looked at Hunter quizzically.

"Never mind." Hunter checked the GPS tracker and looked for Harold's phone's location. "That-a-way..."

CHAPTER 8

RETURNING THE FAVOR

Margaux marveled at how Hunter could follow a trail, even without the aid of her computerized glasses. The Task Force agent saw physical clues that she would never have seen. Hunter stopped and knelt to look at a bush. She lowered her glasses from atop her head for a detailed view of what caught her attention. "I see a trace of cotton-poly on this stem," she announced, "that's the type of pants material Harold prefers, not to say it's his, though." She tapped a small stud on the glasses right wing, which activated different scanner software. "It's only had a couple day's exposure to the elements, so the odds have just increased dramatically." She returned her glasses to the top of her head and fixed her gaze on the nearby ground. "He was still walking alone."

Margaux looked around at all the trees and ground growth, narrowing her eyes trying to feel what her senses were telling her. Hunter noticed her expression. "What?" the agent asked.

"We're being followed."

Hunter stepped to her side, putting her glasses back on. "My heat-resolution view doesn't show anything. How far away are our followers?"

"I'm not sure, Hunter, I'm sorry. I feel a... disturbance in the air."

"Interesting. I feel nothing myself. No, don't be sorry." Hunter put both hands on Margaux's shoulders. "Be my rear guard. You say you're a sensitive, and your record says even more. I'm concentrating on where we have to go; you make sure we're not surprised from behind. That's your job, Chocolate."

"Yes, ma'am. I will follow a short distance behind if that is okay." She took a deep breath. "Not used to being this high up."

Hunter nodded, and said, "You'll get used to it. You'll actually feel it more in the legs before this is over. We're going uphill now." She turned to resume her pursuit.

Margaux stood in place while Hunter walked forward. Turning around to face the way they came, listening and feeling—feeling threat, anger, help? The opposing sensations confused her, not being able to immediately discern their meaning. She removed her gun from its clip and kept it at the ready, now following Hunter, keenly aware of her surroundings. She reached around to the bottom of her backpack and removed the quick-release canteen to take a swig of water.

Half an hour later Hunter came to a stop and dropped to a crouch again. She held a fist up, signaling Margaux to stop. Margaux studied the area around them but felt nothing. Hunter reached around to her backpack and withdrew a metal cylinder from a lower opening. Without moving from her position, she studied the ground carefully: broken twigs, unnatural indentations in the ground, displaced fallen leaves. "There was a struggle here."

"Hunter, someone is approaching," Margaux whispered. The sensation was strong, palpable.

Hunter looked up at Margaux and listened. "I don't hear anything," she whispered.

The Whisker silently ran to Hunter's side and crouched behind, so as not to disturb the ground in front. She made a "quiet" motion with her index finger over her lips as they both heard the nearing sound of a vehicle engine above them. They moved backward into the forest, trying to blend in, as it neared quickly, then drove past them before coming to a stop. "There appears to be an unmarked dirt road up there," Hunter whispered. She led Margaux forward as they crept to the top of the incline and looked over it to see an all-terrain vehicle parked about a hundred feet ahead, in front of a small mountain cabin. There were several armed guards of mixed races, all carrying AK47s, and had pistols and knives on their belts.

Seeing the armed guards compelled the two women to be even more aware of their surroundings and remain quiet as instinct and training took hold. Hunter motioned Margaux to move back so they wouldn't be seen. "If I'd known there was a road we wouldn't have had to walk so much," Hunter said. She stared at Margaux, expecting a look of fear, but all she saw was calm. She removed another small box device from a belt pouch and extended a clear fiber-optic antenna, lifting the device up high enough so she could see the activity from the safety of cover. "There's something more going on than just deer hunting," she whispered. "That's a small army squad over that rise. You don't think that much firepower is needed to hunt down a Sasquatch, do you?"

"The ones I know who hunt Sasquatch usually shoot with cameras, not guns." Margaux fiddled with the weapons and instruments on her own belt, assuring she knew where everything was and in place.

"Thought so." Hunter studied the image on the screen. "They seem to be waiting for something."

"What would they be waiting for in the middle of the mountains, Hunter? It makes no sense to me."

"My guess is someone, or something, maybe both. And likely it's something illegal if someone wanted to do this in the middle of nowhere with that much firepower." She looked at Margaux. "Now would be a great time for you to dazzle me with your powers."

"Oh, well, now that you mention it, ma'am, I suggest you roll to your left NOW."

Hunter's eyes widened. The women rolled opposite directions, both taking cover behind large trees. The gunfire started and bullets plucked away at the ground where both had been crouched.

Hunter fired toward the source of the gunfire.

Margaux also returned fire, but toward the cabin where the original guards were now also firing at their position. She wasted no bullets, as she only needed one bullet per opponent to drop them to the ground. "Nice shooting, Tex," said Hunter. "You trying to make me look bad?"

Another vehicle swiftly appeared on the hill and pulled to a stop many yards away. Its occupants got out and, using the doors as shields, began firing toward the women as well. "Hunter, we have company."

"Well, shit, Chocolate, don't stand on ceremony, just drop them. You seem to have a pretty good aim for a Whisker," Hunter replied calmly, despite the hail of bullets.

"You didn't give me more targets to test me, did you, ma'am?" Margaux returned, almost too casually. She released the spent clip from her gun within seconds, loaded a replacement, and continued firing.

Eventually the number of gunshots diminished until finally only Hunter and Margaux were still standing. "Well, that was fun," Hunter said with no emotion. "I'd still like to know what the hell this was all about."

A coughing sound caught Margaux's attention. "There's one still alive, Hunter!" She ran toward the sound of the cough with Hunter right behind. She found a man on the ground behind the vehicle, with a bullet wound in the chest. Blood gurgled from his mouth, his breathing in labored pain. "Talk," ordered Margaux. "What is all this?"

Hunter was taken aback by Margaux's sudden assertiveness but nodded to herself in approval.

"P-pocket," he gasped.

Margaux patted his pants and shirt pockets until she found his wallet, opened it, and looked at the identification. She coldly looked into the man's eyes." Why the hell is the CIA shooting as us?"

CHAPTER 9

THE SURPRISE

"You have what?"

Hunter said to her team leader, Spy, via satellite phone, "A CIA guy apparently was undercover with whatever is going on up here. We were in a massive shootout, he's the only survivor, and that's questionable at this point."

"So, what's his mission?" he asked.

"He passed out. He's pretty bad off. Hoping he'll wake up and give us some answers, unless you can find out first."

"Already checking, Hunter, stand by."

"He's awake, ma'am," Margaux announced.

Hunter knelt beside him again; her cocoons back down to mask her complete identity to him. "I'm from Task Force Division. Why are you here?"

Margaux had grabbed a blanket from the vehicle to prop up his head and chest. Hunter activated the satellite phone's microphone when the man started speaking. "Undercover," he said slowly, trying to suck in air with almost each syllable. "Terrorist cell—bringing in—dirty bomb—target, Seattle."

Hunter said, "Spy, you copy that?"

"Yes. Confirmed what we just got from the CIA, too."

She turned back to the injured agent. "More details?"

He continued, laboring to speak. "Undercover—with transfer team—to relay location here—to identify—whole operation—takedown was planned for—tomorrow—why are you here?"

"Unrelated opp," she replied, "or, at least it was unrelated. Do you know of a Professor Harold Windimer?"

"N-no."

Hunter looked at Margaux. "I'm beginning to suspect that Harold was in the wrong place at the wrong time and got mixed up in this somehow. And, I'm beginning to seriously doubt there was anything supernatural about his disappearance and more likely was captured and hidden away."

"Yes, leaving a dead body around, either on the ground or buried would alter how the wildlife behaves here—and I sense no such disturbance."

Hunter returned her attention to the injured agent. "The bomb? Where are you supposed to be making the pickup?"

"Already—have it. Gas can."

Hunter glanced over at the open vehicle and the contents in the rear. A red plastic five-gallon gasoline container was in clear view. She approached it carefully, adjusting her glasses' view to penetrating sensor. "Oh, shit," she said softly, "Spy, our asses are on a live nuke here..."

CHAPTER 10

A STONE'S THROW AWAY

"We have eyes on it," Hunter communicated to her boss. She said to the CIA agent, "When was the meet to take place?"

"Five o'clock," he wheezed.

"Six hours from now," Margaux said.

"Where?" Hunter asked.

"Here."

Hunter looked at Margaux. "Be on alert. Let's get our CIA friend in the car and to a hospital. You take the nuke back down to the main road, meet up with whichever Division sends to take it off your hands."

"Hunter, what is a dirty bomb anyway? It sounds nasty; I don't think I want to be near it, let alone be driving with it beside me."

"Margaux, didn't they teach you any of this stuff when you were hired?"

"Well, of course I've heard of it, but I've never had reason to know what it was."

"Geez. Okay, it's simple, like that gas can. They've used a small container, doesn't look out of the ordinary like you'd think a bomb would be. It's like, well, it most likely contains TNT packaged with radioactive materials. It's a crude and cheap way to make a nuclear bomb."

"What?" Margaux's French accent became accentuated in her uneasiness. "You want me to drive off with a nuclear bomb, just like it's a little puppy sitting beside me in the car? Vous êtes une idiot!"

"Hey, don't be calling me an idiot, rookie. I know what I'm doing!"

"Je n'ai pas signer jusqu'à être une baby-sitter pour une baise bombe nucléaire," Margaux said angrily under her breath.

Hunter looked over at Margaux, eyebrows wrinkled together. "'Baby-sitter'? You're damn right you're gonna baby-sit this thing, that's our job, Chocolate. Besides, you don't have any reason to worry. The radioactive stuff is meant to be propelled over a wide area. They use it to hurt a lot of people in one big place, like at a football stadium or something. There's alpha and beta particles, gamma rays, and—oh, never mind, now's not the time for a physics lesson. Let's get this man in the truck and you and the bomb to the main road and I'll continue the hunt." She reached down to begin lifting the agent but stopped. "Well, forget that. He's gone." She tucked his wallet in her pack. "We'll send for recovery to pick up him and everyone else later."

"Ma'am, duck!"

Hunter reflexively ducked, narrowly missed being hit by a flying rock to the head. "What the hell? Did you see who threw that?"

"No, ma'am. Maybe the receiving crew is arriving, and they are trying to scare us off, you suppose?"

"No, I don't suppose," Hunter replied. "I think they'd welcome us with another bullet shower..."

CHAPTER 11

THERE AND BIGFOOT AGAIN

Margaux nodded gently in affirmation.

"Before you go, let's try this one more time," Hunter said. She plucked the satellite phone from her belt and turned on the GPS tracker again, looking for the professor's phone coordinates. "Hum, his phone is somewhere nearby." She studied the schematic and looked around. "Just past this cabin, looks like." She walked past the cabin, Margaux following. "Whoa," said Hunter, stopping a dozen feet from the cabin. "My sensor just went blank." She took several steps back and her screen cleared. She tied in her glasses to her sensor and probed the area. "Very interesting. There seems to be a masking electromagnetic field here. That would prevent anyone from picking up the house by ground or atmospheric or satellite radar scan." She turned to Margaux. "And, it would look like a body vanished when viewed from any heat-resolution instrument image." She adjusted her scanner to read for heat signatures as she stepped back into the EM shield. Hunter turned back to Margaux. "I've got a life sign inside the cabin."

Margaux joined Hunter as they approached the cabin door, guns drawn. Hunter reached for the door handle, turning it until it swung inward on its own. She heard a muffled sound as soon as the door opened wide; gun pointed forward, glasses on maximum light resolution, Hunter stepped into the doorway ready to fire—

—but instead saw a middle-aged man sitting bound and gagged in a chair in the middle of the room. Hunter and Margaux scanned the room, carefully approaching the man. "Harold? Oh, thank God we found you!" Hunter and Margaux untied the bound professor. "What the hell happened up here?" asked the Task Force agent.

"Good to see you too, M—" he said, almost letting her real name slip from his lips "—my dear Hunter. And—"

"I am Margaux," said Margaux before Harold could finish.

"Right." Harold smiled and bowed his head, his white hair falling into his eyes. "Well, I was hoping for a rescue but never expected it to be you."

Hunter relaxed on her knees and toes. "It's good to see you, too, Harold. But again, what the hell happened to you?"

"Are we safe here?" he asked.

"For now," Margaux said, earning a quizzical glance from Hunter.

"Well, Hunter, you know me," Harold began, "I can't turn down a chance to find solid physical proof of Bigfoot."

Hunter closed her eyes and shook her head. "Really, haven't you got better work to do at the Smithsonian—and for us?"

He pulled his head back, abashed. "I had vacation time. And there's no rule that says I can't go Bigfoot hunting on my own time."

"He has a point," said Margaux.

"Don't help him," Hunter retorted. "What happened, Harold? How the hell did you end up like this?"

"Well, it was like this." He stood, bending his arms and legs, trying to get his circulation back. He began walking around like he was back in a classroom with Hunter and Margaux as his students. "We received this most incredible video in the archaeology office at the Institute. The video-maker claimed it was of an actual Bigfoot family! And it was the clearest video I'd ever seen, even if it was still a distant-view, of not just one Bigfoot but of two—one big one with a smaller one beside it. It was a Bigfoot child!"

"Would that make it a Littlefoot?" Hunter, still squatting on the floor, asked sarcastically.

Margaux rolled her eyes at the bad pun, and decided it was better for her to stand guard at the door.

"The digital video also had GPS coordinates embedded so I knew exactly where to come to start my own search up here. I found some excellent evidence along my trek up here, perfect Bigfoot proofs of trunk scratches, hair tufts, broken underbrush, even a shelter composed of smaller trees and branches that look perfectly natural at first and even second glance. I found footprints, Mae-Lei," he said excitedly, forgetting to use her codename, earning him a harsh scowl from Hunter, "their footprints! Right outside, not far from this cabin. Two adults, one adolescent or youth. I was starting to take pictures with my camera when—"

"When what?" Hunter asked.

"I was jumped!" he grumbled angrily. "This guy attacked me right in that spot! He forced me to the ground, onto the footprints! He ruined the evidence when he tied me up and forced me in here. Damn him, damn them all!"

"Um, yeah, I saw where you had that struggle," Hunter agreed, "made it easy for me to find this place."

"Why'd it take all this time for someone to get here after I didn't check in on schedule?" he asked. "My phone should still be active, wherever it is—I didn't have it on me when I was searched by them. Who are they anyway?"

"Your phone's still outside somewhere," Hunter replied. "This cabin isn't on the maps; frankly neither is the dirt road leading up here. We hiked up following your signal. And when we found the cabin, we discovered it has an EM shield to hide it from aerial radar."

"Interesting," Harold mused. "But why was I kidnapped? I'm not important to anyone except you and the Institute."

"It wasn't you, Harold. You were in the wrong place at the wrong time."

He looked at her, his brow furrowed in curiosity. "Say what?"

She stood and rested her hands on her gun belt. "You were in the middle of a dirty-nuke transfer operation."

He held his hands behind his back. "They could have just left me alone and gone on about their merry way."

"Criminals aren't that smart, Harold. They probably saw you studying the grounds and figured you were a cop or fed and captured you. They didn't kill you because they didn't want to attract predators or scavengers."

"Logical," he agreed. "But did they have to ruin my evidence? It was the best, clearest evidence ever!"

"Can we get off fantasy and back to reality?" Hunter said exasperatedly. "I'm not here for a wild Bigfoot chase; I'm here to take you home—well, you and that nuke now. Hey, Whisker." Margaux turned back to them. "Your senses telling you we're all clear?"

Margaux cocked her head and stared blankly at her for a few moments. "We are not alone, but we are safe."

Harold smiled, curious who the French woman was and why she was with Hunter.

Hunter fumed. "Okay, this shit's gotta stop. No more of this Bigfoot mumbo-jumbo. Let's get the nuke and get back to the safari. We don't know who else might be out there. We'll make good time, it's all downhill."

Harold quickly moved around the cabin, retrieving all his scientific tools and his own backpack, which had been searched by his captors. "Don't forget my phone, I have notes and photos on it I need for my Bigfoot research," he said.

Hunter looked at her GPS. "What did I just say about your damn Bigfoot silliness? Besides, I can't read it while we're inside the EM's influence. Give me a minute to find the EM generator." She pulled out the scanner and set the frequency search to wide.

"How does that work in here?" Harold asked.

"Not the same as an EM pulse, which disables everything," said Hunter. "Their shield prevents discovery from outside. Ah, there it is." She knelt before the fireplace, waving the scanner slowly over the stone façade until the light on top turned green. She grasped at the brick and easily pulled it free, revealing a control panel within. "No power switch. Oh, well. Cover your eyes, guys." She brought up her pistol and fired once. Immediately her scanner whined. "EM shield is down." She then spoke aloud, "Tactical, got a read on me?"

In her ear she heard, "Loud and clear, Hunter. Lost you for a while."

"Target has been secured. Mark my signal location and send in cleaners and support. Got lotsa crap here, plus most probable incoming terrorist cell."

"Copy, Hunter. Personnel are already en route."

"Gonna need support for our new package, too. We'll be driving outta here with it, coordinate to meet us on the road."

"Also, will be taken care of."

She took Harold by the arm. "Okay, Harold, let's get outa here."

He smiled as he hoisted his pack on the opposite shoulder. "Just like old times, Mae-Lei? And may I say you look exceptionally great in your uniform?"

"Flattery won't get you anywhere," she said, smiling. "Let's go."

Margaux led them out the door to the ATV and stopped when she looked at the back of the truck. "Hunter, we have a problem."

"What?"

"The gas can—it's gone..."

CHAPTER 12

"FOLLOW THE RED"

"Son of a bitch!" Hunter growled as she joined Margaux at the ATV. The gas can was indeed gone. She looked around, even bringing her glasses back down and running full computer sensor scans of their surroundings. She stepped away and checked all the bodies; all were accounted for. "Could we have missed someone during the gun fight?"

"I don't think so," Margaux reported confidently.

"So, where the hell is the nuke?" Hunter demanded. She looked at Harold. "You've seen these guys. Anyone missing?"

He looked around and walked to the various dead bodies. "Nope, looks like you got 'em all."

Margaux saw Hunter's anger starting to grow. She stepped forward and placed a gentle hand on the agent's forearm. "Be calm, Mae-Lei," she said softly. "Relax. Don't think. Be The Hunter, not Mae-Lei. Then you will see the way." She grasped Hunter's other forearm as gently. "It's your time now."

Hunter removed her glasses and looked at Margaux. The Whisker's eyes were glistening…happily. Hunter felt her anger disappear the longer she held eye contact.

"You're in the presence of an old love. Emotions don't die over time; they just get covered over…and occasionally they get uncovered." She took Hunter's gloved hands in her own. "You are The Hunter."

Hunter smiled. "And now Spy is a lot more mysterious now because of you, Chocolate."

"Why must you keep calling me that silly name that Proteus gave me?" Her French accent was more accentuated.

"'Cause it was cute and ridiculous, just like Harold's Bigfoot obsession…why else? If you want a more serious name, file a request with Spy." She reached for her compound bow and an arrow and armed them in her left hand. "Let's go nuke hunting."

"Which way?" Harold asked. "Oh, look! My phone! Thank God!" He stepped several feet away to his phone, which was laying on the ground beside a tree.

Hunter walked the perimeter of the cabin until coming to a stop at a broken bush branch. She looked back at Margaux. "The Way?" Hunter asked, her eyebrows raised in question.

Margaux simply smiled and nodded. She and Harold silently followed Hunter into the trees.

▲

Their path led downward until they came to a break in the trees, a paved road. "Dammit, the trail ends here. If someone picked up our bomber it could be heading anywhere by now."

"Hunter, don't think," said Margaux. Her confidence made Hunter relax again. "You are The Hunter. Don't see the road as a road."

She's right, Hunter thought. *I have to stop thinking about the potential loss of life and concentrate on doing what I do best.* She led them across the road and heard running water. She looked at the vegetation along the road's edge until she found a clue. Without a word she continued forward, with Margaux and Harold following from behind.

They hadn't gone far when they came to a shallow stream with a couple small rapids, one near, and a second a little further south. The sound of the running water was loud, too loud for Hunter. It impaired her ability to hear anything out of the ordinary. On a dry clearing on the opposite side sat the red gas can containing the bomb. It sat, inviting, compelling, but in the open, like a trap, almost too obvious.

"How the hell did it get there?" Hunter asked rhetorically.

Harold shrugged his shoulders, Margaux closed her eyes and grinned slightly. "A friend was trying to help."

Hunter looked at her, her face screwed up in an unbelieving gesture. "'A friend'? What friend? It would've been a lot easier to leave that thing where it was and we'd be handing it off to the bomb experts by now."

"We are not alone," Margaux proclaimed quietly.

Hunter's senses went on full alert. She heard a sound behind her, turned, looked quickly for the source of the sound, drew back her bow, and fired. The natural silence was disturbed by the sound of a falling body up near the road behind them. She drew another arrow, nocked, and prepared to fire as she listened.

Harold tapped Margaux on the shoulder and pointed at the gun on her holster slat. She shook her head back and placed a finger to her lips. He understood that they needed to be quiet.

There was another movement. Through her glasses she saw another man, armed with a rifle. She drew and fired. After twenty years of practice, her arrow was silent and perfectly aimed. He fell instantly when the arrow penetrated his heart. "Geez, where are they all coming from? It's impossible to protect our perimeter," she whispered. "And how the hell are they here without me hearing them?"

"Very excellent aim," said a voice to their side. Three men armed with AK47s aimed at them stepped out of the trees. "Now, drop the bow, Robin Hood, before we drop you…"

CHAPTER 13

SHOWDOWN

Hunter dropped her bow, with its nocked arrow, to the ground. "Guns, too," said the lead man. Hunter and Margaux removed their guns from the holster slats and tossed them to the ground, and the three of them stood with their hands raised. The man, a blond-haired fellow in his late thirties, motioned them to step back while one of his companions stepped forward and picked up the discarded weapons, placing one gun in his waistband while handing the other gun and bow to the other. "Thank you for leading us to our gas can."

"I didn't realize we were leading anyone anywhere," Hunter said evenly.

"You're not the only one who can move quietly through the trees," Blond Man said in a gruff voice. "Used to be Special Forces."

"So, why exactly do you want to be a traitor now?"

He smiled and chuckled. He kicked his boot at the dirt in front of him, and then lit a cigarette, blowing a puff of smoke in Hunter's face. "I don't have to explain anything to you, bitch." He moved closer to Hunter, almost nose to nose. "But I'll tell ya anyway. Money, of course. I'm betting you were also Special Forces or something similar. Those are the only folks I've ever known who can move through the trees like you and me. But you two—" he motioned at Margaux and Harold "—are the loudest trackers I've ever seen."

"So why are you talking us to death instead of just killing us?" Hunter asked.

"Mostly, I was following you because I thought you had our package. I didn't realize 'til now that you were following someone else with it." He looked at the bow in his companion's hand. "You're pretty good with that thing, lady. No idea how you got my guys up there through the trees like you did."

"Lots of practice," she said, angered and impatient, and calculating scenarios of escape.

"Hum," he said. "So, as much as I appreciate you leading us to our property, I'd like to know who brought it all the way down here."

"That makes two of us, actually."

He looked at her and Margaux in their uniforms. "You some kinda cop or something?"

Hunter crossed her arms and smiled a feigned politeness. "Something."

He smiled back. "Yeah, figured you'd say that. Well, as much as I've enjoyed our incredible conversation, we need to dispose of you, so we don't have to worry 'bout you keeping us from our property." He motioned for them to go to the river's edge. "We'll let the water carry your bodies away so no one can find you. How's about that?" He smiled happily; his teeth were yellowed from years of smoking.

"You know we can't let you bomb Seattle," Hunter said, coming to a stop at the water's edge.

Blond Man laughed. "And I suppose you have reinforcements behind us right now, huh, little lady?"

"Nope. Right in front of you."

Blond Man wrinkled his forehead in confusion, looking all around just in case she wasn't bluffing.

She took the opportunity to lift her hands to the quiver still attached to her pack and drew three arrows, two in her left hand and one in the right and flung the single arrow from her right hand as hard as she could. It hit the far-right man in the chest with a soft "thunk", dropping him to his knees and screaming. The distraction was enough to make Blond Man and the third man turn to their wounded companion. Hunter bolted toward them, jumping over a log, her inertia enough to impact the two standing men and dropping all three of them to the ground.

She forced an arrow into the heart of the left-side man with another moist-tissue "thunk", then forced her bow from his dying hand. Blond Man started to stand, and Hunter nocked her third arrow, drew, and fired; but her balance was off on the pebbly ground, and her arrow pierced his shoulder rather than his chest. She charged him and swung her bow like a bat across the side of his head, bone and reinforced wood making a cracking sound, sending him to the ground, unconscious.

Hunter looked across the water. The gas can was still there. "Can we please go retrieve that thing now without anymore interruption?" she asked rhetorically to no one. She waded through thigh-high water to the clearing while Margaux went to the three dead men and retrieved their guns, and the dead men's other weapons.

Hunter stepped out of the water, stopping to listen for any sounds in the forest. She heard nothing out of the ordinary, so she carefully approached the gas can. Dropping to one knee, her glasses' scanners showed it was intact, as was the nuclear bomb inside. She breathed a sigh of relief, until she heard a new voice yell from across the rushing water, "Don't make a move unless you want your friends dead."

Narrowing her eyes, ready for the unknown, she slowly turned her head back. One new lone gunman was holding his own rifle at Harold and Margaux. "You drop that bow like a good little girl and bring back that can."

Hunter said aloud, "You know, this shit's really getting old. I had better plans to celebrate my birthday."

"I could give a shit about your birthday, bitch," he yelled back. "Bring that can or your pals here get their brains blown out."

The data readout in her lenses gave her distance readings, wind speed, temperature, even the minute pressure variation over the water as opposed to the dry ground. He had her companions in point-blank range, and as good an archer as she was she knew she couldn't arm and fire before he could kill them both.

A loud high-pitched whooping sound echoed in the trees back up toward the road. The sound was loud enough to make the gunman turn his attention to the unusual sound. That gave Hunter plenty of time to draw a shaft, nock, draw, and fire—hitting him square in the carotid artery. He attempted a silent scream from the pain and dropped to the ground, dying rapidly.

She attached the bow to its clip on her pack, lifted the gas can gently, and carefully walked back through the water to Margaux and Harold. "I'm impressed," she said to them. "How did you make that sound?"

Margaux and Harold looked at each other, then at Hunter. "We didn't," Margaux said.

"Then who did?..."

CHAPTER 14

"WAY"

Local police had the road blocked off while Task Force personnel secured the riverfront scene, assisted by Homeland Security and the FBI. The gas can nuke was taken away by Marine helicopter to be disposed of based on standard military procedures. The bodies at both the cabin and the riverside were gathered by Task Force and Homeland personnel working together.

Hunter was dictating her report on her audio recorder when a Bell jet helicopter landed on the river clearing. Everyone ducked slightly, covering their eyes with their arms as the dirt and dust settled from the rotors. Agent Spy, dressed in his full black uniform, stepped out of the opened door, walking over to Hunter, Margaux, and Harold. He shook each of their hands when he joined them. His filtered voice said, "Well, Harold, it looks like you accidentally put us in the middle of a true national security incident."

"That wasn't my idea," he said, smiling, "but I was definitely rescued by the best ladies in the world."

"Yes, they are definitely that," Spy agreed as he nodded his head. He pointed back at the helicopter. "Harold, that chopper will take you back for debriefing."

"You're all not coming?" he asked.

"Not right now," Spy replied. "Have a safe trip."

Harold extended his hand to Margaux. "It was very good to meet you, Margaux."

Margaux simply smiled and stepped away. Harold then spread his arms to embrace Hunter. "One hug for an old friend?"

Hunter smiled and accepted his embrace. "You're not old," she said in his arms.

"I'm available if you are," he whispered softly in her ear. His unshaven face tickled her cheek.

"Yeah, thanks for the offer, Harold," she replied as she pulled away, "but I'm not, well, y'know, I'm just not ready yet."

Harold nodded his head. "I understand, my beautiful friend." He offered his hand to Agent Spy, who shook it. "I remain in your service, sir. Thank you for the rescue, and I do apologize for such a ruckus. Believe me, that certainly wasn't what I came here for."

Spy said, "Let's not make a habit of it, okay? Besides, if you'd not gone missing, we'd not known about this group and their terrorist plans. So, you did us a favor by almost getting yourself killed."

"Ah, yeah, I'll be planning my expeditions a little more carefully next time, you can count on that!"

Spy replied, "Oh, and if you get anymore mystery videos, let us check it out first before you go exploring?"

Harold shook his head emphatically, "It's a deal." He picked up his pack from the ground and walked to the waiting helicopter. "By the way, Mae-Lei—happy birthday." He gave a two-finger salute and boarded the aircraft. The choppers engine roared louder and louder until it slowly began hovering upward, then picked up speed as it flew away. Spy and Hunter watched until it was out of sight.

"Speaking of 'way'," Hunter said as she and Agent Spy caught up to Margaux, "just what the hell was all that about?"

"Ah, I see you've been getting to know our Whisker very well," he said. When they joined her he said, "I've come to learn that this young lady is far more than she appears. You've probably already come to learn that when she says something it's best to do exactly what she says."

"Well, you have been an interesting companion, to say the least," she said to Margaux. She saw the Whisker's eyes focus on hers for a moment. "Oh, geez, what now?"

"I suggest you stay right behind Spy."

"Why?"

Margaux said softly, "Follow the red. Ignore, be dead."

Hunter looked at her and then at Agent Spy, totally confused. "But, he's not red. He's dressed in black," She whispered as she looked for something else out of the ordinary.

Margaux ignored her and waited for Hunter to start walking.

Several steps later, as they neared the tree line by the river clearing, Hunter heard a whistling sound in the air and instinctively moved forward next to Spy's back. A rock hurtled between her and Margaux and would have hit Hunter in the neck had she not moved reflexively. She looked at the rock when it landed over twenty feet away and rolled even further on the ground toward the water. She drew her pistol as she studied the direction that the flying rock came from. "What the hell? Where the hell did that come from?"

Hunter stepped away from her companions and aimed her pistol toward the probable source of the rock…standing completely still with her mouth agape in disbelief. She slowly lowered her weapon as she stared in complete astonishment. "Oh—my—God." She turned to Margaux and Spy. "Did you see that?"

"See what?" Spy said as he looked where Hunter pointed.

"That!" She turned back—and saw nothing. "It's gone!"

"What's gone?" Spy asked.

"It was—it was a—" Hunter couldn't put a complete sentence together. "Chocolate, tell me—no way—"

The Cat Whisker stood proudly with her shoulders pulled back. Her bearing was of satisfaction. "Yes, 'way'." She shook Hunter's hand. "It was a great honor to work with the legendary Hunter of Task Force." Margaux smiled. "I look forward to our next mission together." Before Hunter could respond she stepped over to Spy and pressed her hand against his chest. She looked up into his black-lensed eyes and said, "Still red." With one last smile she started to walk toward the team of investigators but stopped and addressed them both. "Your eyes are open now, Hunter, as are all possibilities for you. Take your time, let it set in. Spy, I will be back when you are black." She turned and walked away from the agents.

Hunter placed her hand on Spy's chest. "'Red'? What does that mean?" she asked.

"She once said my heart was red, and that one day it would be black, or something like that," he said.

"'Follow the red. Ignore, be dead', she said. If I hadn't followed you just then that rock would have hit me in the head; it could have killed me."

"I think you should consider a different definition of that statement." He gave her a gentle pat on her shoulder and stepped away.

Hunter stood alone at the tree's border, looking back up into the shadows, searching and contemplating what she thought she had just seen and what Margaux had said. Then she heard a soft guttural sound somewhere before her, but she didn't feel threatened; she felt very comfortable.

A small stone came out of the trees, gently hit the ground, and landed right at her toes. Hunter looked at the stone for several seconds, contemplating the aim and skill required to toss a stone to land precisely and gently at her feet. She finally smiled in understanding, realizing she was never in danger. She looked back into the trees and waved once, then left the trees to join her team leader…

▲

…a large dark figure disappeared into the shadows of the trees…

ABOUT THE AUTHORS...

JACK GANNON

Jack Gannon began his literary career with high school best friend Cyndi Williams-Barnier after they were both retired from their respective careers, writing the stories they talked about way back in high school.

YBR Publishing was born when Jack wrote and published his first solo book, "I WALKED IN SANTA'S BOOTS", a coffee-table-sized autobiography about his quarter-century as Santa Claus for Beaufort, SC. "SANTA" was entered into the Beaufort County Library Historic District Collection as an important book reflecting the history of Beaufort, SC, as well as the Columbia State Library as an important book in South Carolina history.

His decades in print media gave him the experience to put together that first book in a unique and attractive scrap-book style, and now serves as the Production Manager for YBR Publishing. Jack works one-on-one with each author to create a distinctive visual signature in the book from cover to cover, a trademark style individual to each author with YBR Publishing. In addition, Jack is YBR Publishing's webmaster and finance manager.

Jack also serves on the Liturgy Committee for St. Peter's Catholic Church in Beaufort as its chairman and the Proclaimer Ministry chair.

He is retired from The Beaufort Gazette & The Island Packet after 24 years in management plus another ten years prior as a motor route delivery carrier and intern reporter.

In January 2021, Jack was double honored by Marquis Who's Who with inclusion in the Marquis Who's Who Top Executives and the Albert Nelson Marquis Lifetime Achievement Award for his lifetime careers in print media and publishing.

Jack lives in Beaufort, SC, with his wife Mendy; Tasia, a 15-year-old Pomeranian; and Mister Grey, an 8-year-old Russian Blue who is "a lot of cat"!

CYNDI WILLIAMS-BARNIER

Cyndi Williams-Barnier, a Beaufort, South Carolina native, brings to YBR Publishing 25 years of county government service in Emergency Management, including writing and managing grants, writing training programs and detailed multi-agency operations manuals for disaster preparation and recovery. Her detailed programs are still used as guideposts for county, state and federal agencies including FEMA, Homeland Security and the National Guard at the Pentagon.

As co-founder of YBR Publishing and co-author of nine books, she brings a unique personal perspective and experience to maximize marketing opportunities for YBR and its authors. Her eye for detail and creative skill brings the emotional connection to every manuscript.

Cyndi was awarded a plaque and flag flown over Camp Phoenix, Afghanistan, from the Department of Defense; plus, she was awarded a retirement plaque from the Beaufort (SC) County Emergency Management Division for her 20 years of service.

Cyndi lives in Ridgeland, SC, is married to Bill and has one adorable cat, Scooter (who serves as her personal YBR critic)!